THE CHRISTMAS WREATH

THE GRAND VOYAGE

DR. DAWN MENGE

Table of Contents

Introduction

She could hear the snow softly falling as she started a cozy fire. Christmas Eve used to be so full of children, excitement, and exhaustion. The wonderful kind of exhaustion that comes from raising a young family and being able to share the magic of Christmas. She curled up on the couch bundled in the new blanket her daughter had made for her. Smiling quietly as she closed her eyes, taking herself back to the warm memories of her children and Christmas Eve nights. She was a grandma now, relinquishing holidays to her children's in-laws and learning to cherish her newfound independence. She was learning to enjoy the solitude that being single was bringing her. Smiling, she drifted off to sleep to dream sweet dreams of a future not yet known to her.

CHAPTER ONE

The Mysterious Christmas Wreath

Christmas morning was chilly with a few inches of newly fallen snow blanketing the mountains. Harmony loved the smell of pine trees and her small town. She had moved back to Wrightwood when she divorced after a thirty-year marriage which brought her three wonderful children. Her children had blossomed into thriving successful adults, married, and lived close. Harmony felt so lucky to have them near as she had been gifted with six beautiful grandchildren. Three boys and three girls. The perfect combination of tea parties, motorcycles, and traveling adventures. This Christmas she was spending with her daughters, son, and their families at her favorite middle child's house. This being a familiar family tease, naming her children her favorites based on their individuality. Her favorite oldest daughter, her favorite middle child, and her favorite son.

She needed to get moving to pack up all the Christmas goodies she had collected. Harmony stretched her toes out under the blankets to test the chill in the air. She quickly snuggled back under the blanket to gather herself to brave the cold mountain air.

"One, two, three…." Harmony sang to herself as she jumped up, throwing the blankets to the floor, and ran to turn the heat up. She did not have time to stroke the fire to life to warm the house. Despite growing up in the beautiful small town of Wrightwood and spending her youth walking barefoot in the snow, she found that she was not as fond of the snow and cold as she used to be. She had gone from a young woman who loved skiing night and day to a grown woman who enjoyed watching the snow fall, drinking hot chocolate, and cuddling by the fire.

Harmony was soon dressed in her pink sweater, Levis, and snow boots. She had gathered her Christmas treats, gifts, and car keys and headed outside to her car. As she drove slowly out of town, she loudly sang Christmas Carols perfectly content with her life and the day ahead. The forty-minute drive was filled with old classics and many new carols. Even if she didn't know all the words, she continued to hum her way through them. The roads were quiet and serene, and Harmony soon reached her destination.

"Grandma, Grandma I'm so glad you are here!" Chimed in the youngest of the grandchildren. "What did you bring us?" The three youngest gathered her packages and placed them under the Christmas tree. Harmony had made sure they were not breakable this year knowing that the children would shake them trying to guess what was inside. A round of hugs and kisses were given to everyone as they gathered in the kitchen to help with the finishing touches. Harmony took a big whiff in and savored the tantalizing smells of turkey, and ham cooking in the oven. "It all smells so yummy! What can I do to help?"

"Can you whisk the mashed potatoes while I set everything out?" her daughter Hope asked her as she peeked her head out from behind the cupboard door. "I'd love to." Harmony grabbed the whisk and fluffed up the potatoes watching her other children happily laughing and putting all the food out.

"Christmas dinner is ready guys!" Hope called out to her family. The stampede of the family to be the first to sample the delicious dinner was loud and filled with love. Harmony knew how wonderful life was for her during these moments of family togetherness. Dinner was filled with lively conversation, planning for the next vacations, and catching up on family matters. Soon, tummies were filled and dishes were in the sink. It was time for everyone's favorite part, the opening of the gifts.

All you could hear was ripping paper, squeals, and sounds of delight. "I've been wanting this forever, Mom." or "How did you know I wanted that?" Harmony and Annie, her oldest granddaughter, had bought warmie blankets for everyone in the family. They had gotten the idea from a Halloween camping trip and decided everyone needed one. Annie had done all the choosing and wrapping. A very big job that she handled with ease.

The day flew by, and darkness soon arrived. "I'd better be heading home; it is supposed to snow again tonight," Harmony announced as she began hugging and kissing everyone goodbye. She continued to sing Christmas Carols on the drive home as Christmas was not over until the clock hit midnight.

Just as she was arriving in her driveway a soft snow had begun to fall. She was thankful she had another week off to relax and get snowed in. She loved her Christmas breaks to rest and relax. Teaching students with severe cognitive delays was her passion but she needed time for herself to recharge. Harmony discovered that she had forgotten to turn on the porch light. As she was slowly walking towards the door her shoe kicked something.

"What is that?" she wondered, reaching inside to turn on the light. Harmony reached down and picked up a beautiful Christmas wreath. It must have fallen off of the door. I wonder where it came from. She took it inside for further inspection.

"What a beautiful wreath." She whispered to herself. It was filled with red velvet ribbons, Christmas holly, and little bells. Harmony found two silver bracelets attached to the wreath and a small white envelope. She opened it slowly.

It read, "You have been invited to spend two nights at the famous Queen Mary. Pack your finest clothes and check in at the front desk on December 31. You will begin a new journey filled with magic, adventure, and the deepest love possible." There was no signature.

Harmony hung the wreath on her hearth after removing the beautiful antique bracelets and headed to bed. She was completely perplexed but very curious about this utterly mysterious wreath and the invitation to her unknown future.

CHAPTER TWO

New Year's Eve and the Queen Mary

Harmony as usual was snowed in the week between Christmas and New Year's. She had spent the week catching up on her favorite vampire show, indulging in long naps, and warm baths, and watching the flames of the fireplace dance shadows onto the mysterious Christmas Wreath. She really enjoyed so much being able to become snowed in and not worry about shoveling or trying to get out. This was her time to pamper herself, and catch up on her writing and TV shows. Many hours were spent trying to figure out who had placed such a beautiful wreath on her door. Her address was not commonly known as she had had trouble with a stalker for years and kept her private life as private as possible, including her location.

Harmony was one for adventure and spent the next week packing and unpacking for her trip to the Queen Mary. What should she wear to her mysterious rendezvous? The Queen Mary was a famous ocean liner whose heydays were in the 1930s and '40s. Harmony had never been there but had always wanted to go. Visions of roaring 30's flapper dresses, movie stars, and the elite of both Europe and the U.S. traveling the ocean in the historic ship wove through her mind.

As the week progressed, she became more excited but was also filled with apprehension. Before she knew it, the day had arrived. New Year's Eve morning was storm-free, the sun was shining, there were no clouds in sight and her driveway and street had been plowed, allowing her easy access to drive out to her mysterious man.

Harmony looked out the window, gathered her courage and her bag, and stepped out into the bright sunshine. The snow glistened with freshness, and it gave her a sense of happiness. No matter what happened in the next few days she knew deep inside that she would never be sorry for embarking on this unknown adventure.

Her drive was smooth, and she soon turned into the parking lot of the famous ocean liner. She was not prepared for the vastness inside the harbor. The ship had been placed into the harbor many years before and turned into a hotel filled with hauntings and stories of the past. Harmony was intrigued by the historical stories and was determined to stay even if her mysterious man had changed his mind. She had researched the ship before going and had chosen a few tours to learn about its history. If nothing else, she would write a story about the ship's adventures. In Harmony's spare time, she wrote children's stories on her family adventures and was ready to expand her writing skills.

Harmony entered the loading area and stopped to watch a movie on the history of the ship. She also needed to gather herself to be ready for either the biggest event of her current life, or the biggest unsolved mystery, of the Christmas Wreath. The film ended and she took a deep breath, pushed the button on the elevator, and floated up three floors. Exiting the elevator, she was taken back eighty years and entered the area where the guests checked in. She could feel the history within the wall of the exquisitely decorated entranceway. She bravely walked up to the counter and asked for her room key. She had closed her eyes expecting to be told she was not on the roster, but the clerk smiled brightly, "Ms. Harmony, we have been waiting for your arrival. You have our best suite, and your benefactor has asked that you charge your meals and whatever else you would like onto your room, and he will take care of everything."

"Oh my, thank you so much! That is so generous." With shaking hands, Harmony took the key, picked up her bag, and began to find her room. She stopped for a moment and turned to the clerk. "Is there a note for me?"

"Yes, I almost forgot. He said to open it up tonight at midnight." The clerk smiled with a twinkle in her eye as she handed Harmony a small white envelope with a little heart keeping it closed.

"Thank you, I will follow his instructions." Harmony continued down the long, crooked hallway and soon found her suite. There were red roses shaped like a heart on the bed. The room smelled of lavender. Two bouquets of red and white roses were placed on the nightstand, and a gift basket filled with bath scents, chocolates, and champagne topped the pillows.

Feeling a little overwhelmed, she gathered all the rose petals, filled her bathtub with hot water, poured the lavender bubble bath into the warm water, and sprinkled the rose petals into the tub. She lit the candles that were in the basket, turned the bathroom lights off, gracefully lowered herself into the tub, closed her eyes, and drifted off into a luxurious dream.

The cold water woke Harmony from her dream filled with her and her mysterious man aboard the Queen Mary II. In the faded shadows of her dream memory, she could see herself in a white dress, and he was in a black tailored suit. They were so happy, giggling and laughing, walking along the deck just as the sunset was fading into the vast ocean. Their hands were intertwined, swinging slowly as they stopped by the railing for a long passionate kiss. He brushed her hair aside and kissed her forehead. "My Queen, you are finally aboard a ship meant just for you and me." His voice was so familiar. In the moments between sleep and being fully awake, she tried to recall how she knew the voice.

"Oh, I'm so hungry. I need to find some dinner." Harmony jumped out of the tub, hastily dried herself off, and dressed for a light snack in the bar. The experience itself was amazing. Harmony felt immersed in days gone by. The music was fit for the time period, her drink was named, "dancing flappers" and she felt completely at home in her new surroundings. The evening flew by, and everyone was getting ready for the big event. It would soon be midnight, the dawn of a new year. For Harmony, a whole new adventure was looming on the horizon.

She stayed with the other guests in the bar, celebrating the night. She felt strangely as if she was in the exact place that she needed to be. Merriment and laughter filled the air. She stayed until it was almost time to ring in the New Year. She looked and looked in her sequined bag but could not find her envelope.

"I must have left it in the room." She hurried back just in time to open it up at the stroke of midnight. With trepidation, she slowly opened the envelope, took the card out, and read, "My love, to our new beginnings. This year will bring you happiness beyond your imagination, love beyond compare, and the union we have always dreamed of. Love, your Huggy Bear"

Harmony almost fainted. Huggy Bear, this was the man who the women had stalked and harassed her over. They had parted ways in all the chaos that they created. Could it be possible? Was this really the man she had fallen for on his first phone call? His voice had reminded her of her father. She felt an instant connection to him.

Maybe, this was a cruel joke from these two women? They thrived on making her life a living hell and trying to not only destroy her life, and relationship with this man, but also her sense of safety. It had taken her years to recover both emotionally and financially. She had continued to show him they were following her, but he had never responded.

Harmony slept a restless night that night. Not knowing how to feel about her mysterious wreath and trip to the Queen Mary. But her dream was so real. She suddenly knew, his was the voice that was in her dream. She felt a warmth envelop her and she knew that no matter what happened, she was safe and loved by this man.

CHAPTER THREE

The Grandest Ocean Liner

Harmony awoke on the first day of the new year with so many questions and very few answers. Not one to like being unsure of her life, she decided to let the unknown stay unknown for now. Before coming on her trip, she had booked several tours. There was the history of the voyages, a short haunting tour, and then later tonight a séance of the ghosts who haunted the halls of the majestic boat.

Harmony, dressed in jeans and a sweater, grabbed a quick sandwich at the coffee shop and barely made it in time for her first tour. The grand ballroom was covered in gold inlay, magnificent fireplaces on both ends, and mirrors adorned the walls. There were pictures of famous passengers ranging from actors, actresses, producers, and even presidents.

Harmony learned of the different classes of the ship's voyages, that the hallway was indeed bowed due to the construction of the ship, it prevented it from breaking in half during rough seas. The staircase located on the third level that many passengers died on when the ship hit a big wave. The sailor who was crushed in the emergency room, and the little girl who drowned in the pool and continued to haunt the hallways looking for her mother. Harmony was so fascinated by the stories and history of the ship she became immersed in the tours, taking notes as she walked from one end to the other. The Queen Mary was built in Scotland and in 1936. On its maiden voyage across the ocean, it carried mail from one continent to another.

By late afternoon Harmony's feet ached from walking, she had lost count of how many stairs she had climbed up and down, making sure that did not miss a single inch of history on the ship. After lunch she sat in Winston Churchill's desk chair in his suite. He had spent many voyages traveling on the grand ship, and she could still smell his cigar smoke lingering in the curtains and walls. She closed her eyes and imagined him giving orders and having secret meetings with his staff. Oh, how she wished she had been able to be part of that life so many years ago.

CHAPTER FOUR

The Grand Ballroom

After a quick nap, Harmony dressed in her newest outfit. She had thought it only fitting to wear a Flapper dress just like the women of high society who had traveled on the Queen Mary.

Having been single for a while Harmony was not concerned about eating alone. Even in such a grand hotel. Harmony even enjoyed it a little more on the first day of this new year. She wanted to feel the environment that her secret admirer had given to her. There was a purpose to this, she just didn't know what it was yet. She didn't want to waste a single moment of such a special time worrying about the unknown.

Dressed in her finest flapper attire she went to the dining room. It was all she had imagined. The headwaiter dressed in a tux seated her by the big picture window, the city lights sparkled in the background, a candle illuminated the table as a glass of their finest wine was poured for her. Whoever was providing this amazing experience was silently softening her heart to the promise of magic for the upcoming year.

Before Harmony was able to look at the menu the waiter brought her meal with all her favorites. Her steak was cooked to perfection, tiny carrots and potatoes cooked just enough to be soft, salad with beets and croutons, freshly made sourdough bread covered in butter lightly laced with honey to top off her meal. After her day of walking, she was famished and finished every bite.

When she was finished, the waiter brought another small envelope. Harmony's heart sank just a little bit. I knew this was a dream that was too good to be true, here is the bill. She slowly opened the envelope that was sealed with a small heart, just like the other two.

To her amazement sand spilled out onto her lap, three small seashells and a sand dollar were soon to follow. The note read,

Love letter....😍
Here are just ten things about you that I love.....
first you are sexy,
second you are intelligent,
third you are photogenic - that last picture you took of yourself and
sent to me on my phone was hot...
fourth you are passionate - about work, her writing, her kids, her
friends just to name a few
fifth you have the most sexy laugh -- it drives me crazy to hear you
laugh ....
sixth you are a very beautiful women -
seventh you have a very nice smile
eighth you are a very good lover
ninth you are very confident of who you are
tenth you are financially independent

Harmony almost fell out of her seat. This was the love letter Scott had sent her when they first met. How could anyone have that information? The bad women had hacked into all of her emails. Maybe they saw it? They were cruel enough to pull a stunt like this.

Harmony gathered up the sand and seashells and placed them back in the envelope. She gently placed it in her purse and headed off to the

Grand Ballroom to listen to music. Her heart was telling her that everything was going to be just fine.

The ballroom was softly lit, and the band was playing a jazz song from the 1930's. Harmony had a sudden surge of déjà vu. She'd been here before. Standing exactly where she was standing. But a man was standing next to her. She was dressed in white, and he was wearing a suit. They had danced the night away in this very room. This room was in her dream. The dream she had when she had first arrived at the Queen Mary. Harmony felt a little dizzy, she began to sway and sat in the closest chair. There she stayed for several hours. Not even aware of the passing of time. She felt as if she had been transported to another place, a place set in the past but was actually in her future. What was happening in her life?

<u>CHAPTER FIVE</u>

Beginnings of Love

Harmony returned to her stateroom and slept soundly that night. She was not disturbed by dreams of the unknown. She had settled into a state of warmth and safety. She was not even sure why. This was the strangest experience she'd had in her whole life. This connection she had formed with Scott. The first night they had spent together he had climbed to the top of a mountain and prayed for their connection under a huge cross. Harmony had been unaware of this until years later. She was getting a massage and her masseuse mentioned they had walked to the top of Mr. Rubidoux for Easter service. Harmony had looked up the Mountain and discovered the cross. Her love had prayed for their connection before they made love for the first time. Their union was explosive. She had never felt such a strong connection with a man as she felt with him.

They made love over and over again that night. It seemed that they couldn't get enough of each other. Her nickname for him emerged that night. He was raised in the city and was unfamiliar with mountain animals. He teasingly kept asking if a bear was going to come up on the porch. They hugged tightly and Harmony assured him that a bear could not get on the porch. They soon returned to their lovemaking until the sun rose. His nickname was born that night: "Huggy Bear".

Harmony lingered in her bed in her suite in the Queen Mary with memories of Scott floating through her mind. Her connection with him was always so very special even from the very beginning. They met on a dating site. Something Harmony had sworn she would never do. But her friend at work wanted her to learn to talk to men. She'd been married at nineteen and it lasted for almost thirty years. Dating was not something she had done a lot in high school. Newly divorced, she really didn't know what she wanted out of her life. Her children were grown, she had a good job, and she loved to travel.

Scott had contacted her on this dating site. She remembers the first time he had called. She was sitting in her dad's favorite chair getting ready for work. She was living with her mom saving her money to buy her own house. He called her as he was walking to work. She could hear his footsteps as he was talking on her voicemail. It wasn't what he said, but the feeling she got when she heard his voice. It reminded her of her father. Her father was someone who was strong, handsome, intelligent, and dedicated to his family. She still felt his love even though he had been gone for twelve years. Some people exist in this world who leave a presence in your heart even though they are no longer walking with us on earth.

Their first date was breakfast at the Grizzly Bear. She felt immediately drawn to him and they went on a twelve-hour date. She had never gotten in a car with a man she did not know. He was different and she knew he would keep her safe. They had a wonderful time, and they didn't want it to end. They went to museums, botanical gardens, and tar pits. He drove her home the long way, up the winding mountain road which was the back way to her house. They stopped at Inspiration Point to look out over Los Angeles below. On a clear day, you can see Catalina Island. He braved a short kiss on her lips. She giggled and felt like she was a teenager again. They held hands as he drove her back to the restaurant where she had left her car that morning. Harmony remembered not wanting to say Goodbye, not wanting the date to end.

They continued to have amazing conversations; she could always feel his presence around her even when he wasn't around. They talked for hours, and in a short time, their conversations moved to marriage. Getting married on the beach, surrounded by the ocean sounds that she so loved. She had even picked out a flowing white dress that would have been perfect for a beach wedding. She sent him the picture and their conversations became deeper and their closeness tightened. She would text him fun little romantic scenes with pictures of G-strings attached. Tantalizing his imagination, he would answer the stories with his own adventuresome ideas. Harmony remembered the first time he took her to his house. It was early in the relationship, and they had gone to the movies. He lived in Redlands, a town she was not too familiar with. She had gotten married in a mansion there, but that was so long ago. He drove her up a winding road to his castle on top of the hill. She immediately fell in love with his home. She had a moment when she thought he didn't live there. She saw a portrait of him and his brothers on the wall and they all looked alike. He was exactly as he said he was. She let her feelings for him grow at that moment. His house felt like her grandmother's house. A home filled with class, intelligence, and love. There was so much love inside that house that you were surrounded by it. They had so many memories shared together in that home.

CHAPTER SIX

The Dark Fog Envelopes Their Love

A few months later he asked Harmony to move in with him and his mother, who he was caring for. She would have moved in a heartbeat, but her ex was acting out and she became scared. She told him no, fearing he would hurt Scott. Harmony was so sad that night, she tried to explain to him, that she really wanted to be with him, but sadly, there were issues.

Their love grew deeper but there was darkness lingering at the edges. A darkness she couldn't quite put a finger on. It was something that wasn't attached to him but rather around him. It was the first time she had felt such a strong darkness. She couldn't explain it but it was there. She would soon find out why she was feeling this darkness.

Scott was part of a ministry, and he wanted her to meet his ministry partner. On the other hand, she thought going to a women's group would help her heal from the abuse she had suffered at the end of her marriage. But Scott said that he really wanted to know what his ministry friend would say to a woman he was dating and so she agreed.

Harmony sent a text to this ministry woman, and then she invited her friend Rose to come over also. At first, it seemed the ministry woman was friendly, talking to Harmony's children, laughing that they both had the same car. Harmony gave her a tour of her house and told her all about her children's books. She showed her the beautiful mural her illustrator had painted on her bedroom wall. She awoke each morning to the lava tubes, sea turtles and her father's sailboat beautifully colored from pictures she had taken from her many trips to Kona, Hawaii. She took her into her office and they discussed Harmony's children's books. She showed the church woman her family pictures displayed on the walls of her many adventuresome vacations which Harmony's books were created from.

But it soon turned bizarre. The ministry woman said that she could get Harmony's Scott to marry her whenever she wanted and snapped her fingers. This was shocking news to Harmony as Scott and she were very involved with each other and planning their future together. The ministry woman spent hours sitting in Harmony's home talking about her Scott in a negative manner, talking badly about their church friends, and saying very strange things about religion. Harmony sat quietly not intervening. She did not see a reason to correct this woman's thoughts. She did not know who she was and assumed she would never see her again. Harmony soon just zoned out and stopped listening to her.

When Harmony finally mentioned to the ministry woman that Scott had asked her to meet me so she could attend the women's group, the church woman started to threaten Harmony. She pointed outside her house and said she had been sitting in front of her house in the middle of the night and was walking around putting a trail of blood around Harmony's house. The ministry woman said, "He wants a Dragon Slayer who looks good in a thong and I'll never let that happen."

Harmony promptly thanked her for coming and walked her out. Harmony began thinking of the ministry woman as the "Church Woman". That was the start of being terrorized and harassed in her home for many years. They continued to harass Harmony until she was forced to sell her home and live with her son. After a year Harmony bought another house at the urging of Scott. This home was in a gated community and had security. He told her to get a restraining order on the Crazy Church Lady, but Harmony was too afraid to do it on her own. She thought all the evilness was over and they could start their relationship anew. He had marked it on his calendar that September first was their new beginning.

Scott came over and they had an amazing time in her new home. The passion and love was still there. But then he told her he had made pictures that looked like the ocean that she could hang in her bedroom. At this point, Harmony got the feeling that he was trying to replace the mural on her bedroom wall that she had loved for so many years. She spiraled down into despair.

After he left, she Googled his name to find his paintings. She came upon a woman he had mentioned that was his friend. Harmony had thought this woman was no longer part of his life. His mother had told her that the crazy church lady had ended their friendship. So Harmony called her, thinking that they had both been hurt by this woman and that maybe she could help her get a restraining order. They talked all night, and Harmony explained what had happened to her. Harmony didn't expect this woman to scream and threaten her, but that was what happened.

Harmony became even more afraid after that phone call. The woman did not act right. Harmony soon found out she had actually found the hornet's nest. She had found the puppet master who was the source of all the terrible things that had happened to her and that would continue to happen. Harmony became so afraid that the terrorizing would start again in her new home that she asked Scott to change his number so that these women would not know that they were talking. These women had invaded all of Harmony's life. Harmony and Scott continued to email each other through an account she made especially for him. Harmony eventually spoke with a detective, and the detective told her to never let the church lady find out where she lived.

The Barn Woman continued to stalk and harass her online for five more years. Harmony gave up the home that she had purchased for her and her Huggy Bear and returned to her mountain community. Harmony also discovered that an author who had bothered her online was someone that the Barn Woman knew.

Harmony and Scott continued to email, text, and phone each other for several years. Sadly, the harassment continued by the Barn Woman, and she sent so many flying monkeys into Harmony's life, and she just wouldn't stop. Harmony and Scott lost contact and she continued with her life. Her life on her own was always beautiful and filled with family, friends, a career she loved with special needs children, and many adventures. Though she was happy, her life was thriving, and her children's books were impacting people around the world, she still had sadness in her heart. She'd lost her one true love, and she could feel the emptiness in her life for the future they had planned together.

"That's just enough of that!" Harmony said as she brought herself out of the past and back into the present. I must pack and check out. It's time to go home. This weekend has been such an incredible dream filled with love, hope, and adventure. I can't wait to see what this year brings for me.

CHAPTER SEVEN

Love is in the Air

January flew by with snowstorms and shoveling, and Harmony was busy teaching her class of severely handicapped students. There were no more secret messages or presents at her door. Harmony had decided it was all just a strange encounter, one of life's mysteries she didn't have an answer for.

Until the week before Valentine's Day. Harmony started having dreams about her Huggy Bear. Having dreams about him was not unusual for her. She had many of them. But these were very real, and they stayed with her throughout the day. The most memorable was when she was at Scott's house and his mom and dad were there. Harmony and Huggy's dad were in the backyard, and he was telling her how happy he was that his son had found her. These evil women were trying to climb over the fence to get at her and his dad told them to "Get out of here!" Harmony went inside to find her love and she could hear his mom yelling at the Barn Woman telling her to leave them alone and never come back. Scott took Harmony by the hand and led her to his mom's old room. "My mom wants us to have this room. She wants us to share our love here. Just like her and my dad did."

Harmony awoke on Valentine's morning after a splendid dream that her Scott was cuddling with her on the couch and asked her to marry him. She emailed him about her dream, not expecting a reply but needing to express herself anyway.

In her dream, she had come home from work and found red and white roses on her coffee table, a handwritten love letter from her true love with a gorgeous opal ring lying on top. She soon heard a soft knock at the door. When she opened it, there he stood, her long-lost love. They wrapped their arms around each other and started to cry in happiness and joy.

"Stop this Harmony, you need to get to work. It's snowing hard and it's Valentine's Day. You are going to celebrate with your students with a pizza party." Harmony dressed in pink and red wrapped a scarf covered in hearts around her neck and braved the snow. They had a wonderful day at school, and she soon lost track of her dreams.

When she returned home, fresh footprints were leading up to her door. "I wonder who was here. There are no packages…" Harmony slowly opened her door to the fresh scent of roses! Her living room was filled with red and white roses, love balloons, a path of red rose petals, and a white envelope sealed with a heart. It read, "In two weeks, meet me at the castle in the mountains. We will soon be together forever." Harmony fell back on the couch in complete shock. Her Scott was back, and now he would be forever.

"Wait, there's a castle in the mountains? I can't wait to see my Scott again." Harmony took as many of the roses and put them by her bedside as she could. She loved the smell when she woke in the morning. The next two weeks flew by in a whirl of anticipation and excitement.

CHAPTER EIGHT

The Castle in the Mountains

The next two weeks were a mixture of speeding a mile a minute, and then going so slowly that a day felt like a year. Harmony's emotions were making it difficult to concentrate on her students, her writing, and her family. She just couldn't wait to see her love. Thankfully, it had stopped snowing and the days had been unusually sunny and warm. Well, warm enough in the mountains in February. Most of the snow had melted on the streets, and there was just enough to make snowmen with in the yard. This was one of Harmony's funniest memories. When she first moved back to Wrightwood with a friend from work, it had snowed several feet over winter break. Her friend was from Maine and very used to the snow. They decided to have a snowman-making contest. It was something they saw on their local Facebook group. Harmony made a girl all dressed up in boas and hats, drinking wine on her date. Her snowman's counterpart was a good old beer-drinking man having dinner with her very classy snowwoman on the porch. Harmony's friend cheated by spraying paint on him for his clothes. They placed the finishing touch of a vase with flowers on the patio table and laughed at themselves. They had such a marvelous time. Harmony sent a picture of the snowman couple to her Scott and he thought she was so very creative with her winter fun. This memory brought a huge smile to her face.

Harmony was just pulling up to the castle in the mountains. There he was, standing on the porch. He hadn't changed at all. She parked her car and ran up the stairs, she wrapped her arms around him and hugged him like she was never going to let him go. They both began to cry, pouring out the pain and loss from the years of evilness. There they were together at last. They settled down into the soft sofa inside, curled up in each other's arms, not saying a word. At that moment words were not what was important. Just being together and savoring each other's scents. He caressed her hair, planted a soft lingering kiss on her forehead, and said "My forever love…" before they both drifted off into a contented slumber in each other's arms.

That night was filled with slow lingering kisses, exploring long-lost places that hadn't been touched properly since they last saw each other. Just as on their first night together, they made love over and over again. Savoring each other's love as if it was their last day on earth. Never quite getting enough of the kisses, the touches.

Morning rose and hunger moved them enough to leave their love nest and venture out to the place where they had had their first date. With this meal, all their amazing memories flooded back to them. Their favorite memory was when they had taken a trip up to Moonstone Beach. Harmony had found a room right on the beach with a fireplace and a view of the ocean. They took all the back roads on the way there. Scott played romantic music on the way up. They held hands and talked or sat in silence perfectly content in their togetherness. After hours of driving, Scott stopped on top of a hill. Harmony had never seen such beauty. The hillsides were covered in beautiful flowers and the background held the magnificent ocean. She kissed him on the lips and thanked him for showing her such beauty. The wind was howling that weekend, but they still walked on the boardwalk, hand in hand talking about their future together. He said he wanted to retire here, and he drove her around the neighborhood, showing her that he had found the perfect spot. Where the pines met the ocean, they made love. She napped. He took her on a hike through the local national park. When it was time to go they stopped at a local pier to have lunch. They walked to the corner store and bought cookies to take home.

Once in the mountains, they drove through an unexpected snowstorm and shared one of the delicious cookies. He told her it was as yummy as his yummy buns and Harmony's nickname, Yummy Buns was born.

The weekend was filled with walks in the mountains. Harmony shared all of her childhood memories. Growing up in the mountains with a local ski area only a mile away all of the children learned to snow ski and work at the lift. Harmony as a teenager could never resist taking that last ski run. Many times, she ended up skiing home along the Highway when her father grew tired of waiting for her. Scott and Harmony laughed at the memory of Harmony's defiance to a curfew. Where could she have gone? They were surrounded by miles and miles of natural forest. As a grown woman, she understood how fortunate she was to grow up in such a small, close-knit community.

They dined in the local Fancy Dancy restaurant. Sitting close to the fireplace they ordered their favorite meal, which was steak. She treated him to his dinner, taking that moment to spoil him just a little bit. They drove up and down the small narrow streets as she filled him with cherished memories of her youth.

The private country club where they swam in the summer, local areas where they hiked, and the infamous wall where they sat and watched the flatlanders walk the two short blocks of the town.

Their weekend ended all too quickly, sitting and watching the sunset at Inspiration Point. They held each other closely. So much was said in the silence between them. Tears slowly fell from Harmony's face as Scott caressed her. "I will be back soon. I promise. I will come and get you and we will begin our future just as we had planned." He kissed her one last time and drove back down the mountain road. It took Harmony a full hour before she could collect herself and drive back home. She knew she would never be the same after that weekend. Would her Scott return as he promised?

CHAPTER NINE

Moonstone Beach

Harmony felt as if she was living in a dream. A beautiful dream that was finally coming true. Scott texted her good morning and good night every day. He came up as often as he could because he was taking care of his mom who was not doing well. Harmony spent many days and nights at his home with him and his mom. They relaxed by the pool and watched her favorite shows. They made dinner together and made beautiful love together each night. Life was just as it should have been before the stalking began.

They took trips to Vegas, staying in a suite overlooking the strip. Breakfast was served each morning and they looked out over the excitement, content being in the room, and catching up on all the moments they had lost. On their way home he took her through the Valley of Fire. She had never even heard of it and found it to be beautiful beyond measure. They found Petroglyphs, deep, winding canyons, and stunning rock formations. She added it to her list of future books to write.

Harmony had gone camping in Joshua Tree National Park and was writing a children's book on it. Scott enjoyed her passion for children and literature and took her to see his favorite spots. He was an avid photographer and enjoyed finding new and unusual things to capture with his camera.

One especially gorgeous spring day, he showed up at her house and told her to pack her bags. They were off to a special place. Harmony was surprised but happily packed her bags. Her Scott was known for surprising her. Once he took her to a singing road. She did not even know there was such a thing. She loved it so much that she made him drive back and forth over it so she could record it.

He drove for hours playing romance songs and driving through the desert. Harmony began to get a feeling she'd been here before. She reached over and held his hand. Harmony closed her eyes and felt the motion of the car take her onto a journey she had waited years for and survived through hell to get back to. She drifted off into a peaceful sleep not waking until she felt a gentle kiss on her lips. "We are here my love."

We were at the same lodge we had stayed at so many years before. Harmony could not wait to open the door to the exact same room they had stayed in when he'd taken her there to talk about their retirement. He opened the door with a grand gesture and there on the bed was the lovely heart made of rose petals. The room was filled with red and white roses. She turned and grabbed him to squeeze him with all her might. "I just love you so, my Scott!"

He grinned from ear to ear and said, "I love you too! We have so much to discuss. Get some rest and I'll be right back."

Harmony ran herself a hot bath with lavender and sunk into the soothing water. She closed her eyes and nodded off until she felt the water rising above her head. Her Scott had quietly joined her in her bath. She scooted around and he began to wash her hair, gently moving the suds around and gathering them in his hands to rub them around her body. She had never felt so close to him as she did at that moment. They stayed until the water cooled and then made love under the covers with a roaring fire to keep them warm. They were soon fast asleep until morning.

Harmony woke to the bright sunlight shining on her face. Hanging up on the bathroom door was her wedding dress. The one she had picked out when they first began talking about getting married on the beach.

"You must hurry my love. Our wedding will begin promptly at 11 below the Moonstone beach boardwalk. Just as I promised you so many years ago."

CHAPTER TEN

The Wedding

Harmony felt the softness of the dress between her fingers and caressed her face with the lace. It was a white silk floor-length dress with lace at the sleeves and around the collar. It's exactly like the one she had picked out so many years before when she and Scott would stay up all night talking about their beach wedding. She slipped on the dress and twirled around the room. He came over to her and joined in the celebratory dance. They laughed and giggled in excitement, kissing passionately in between twirls.

"I need to do my hair and put my makeup on. You need to skedaddle and give a woman some time to make herself beautiful for you." Harmony stopped her twirling and went into the bathroom, closing the door as she watched him leave the room.

"Anything for you, my Queen. I need to put my suit on and check on the details for our sacred union." He was already halfway out of the bedroom and moving into the parlor. He quickly changed into his suit, made his calls, and double-checked that he still had their rings safely in his pocket.

The weather was as perfect as can be, unlike their first trip there. With the wind howling and them barely able to walk along the boardwalk. The drive was short, and the beach was sparsely populated, giving them the privacy they so desired. Scott helped her out of the car, and they waved to the pastor who was standing at the archway filled with flowers. As the couple reached the sand they bent and took off their shoes. Harmony always wanted a wedding "barefoot in the sand", so she could feel the warm particles between her toes.

"Dearly beloved we are gathered here to join in holy matrimony these two lovers forever and ever" began the pastor. Harmony could hardly understand what he was saying as she was so lost in his intense blue eyes. They locked onto each other and never wavered as they solidified their union. "You may kiss the bride!" the pastor said as he closed the bible. "With pleasure!" Scott said as he grabbed Harmony by the back of the neck and kissed her fully on the lips and then on the forehead. "My forever love!" he whispered into her ear and he took her hand and they walked back up to the boardwalk.

"I am Mrs. Huggy Bear now!" Harmony giggled. "And I am Mr. Yummy Buns!" he said with laughter. They returned to their room to spend the afternoon making love as husband and wife.

"I'm famished, let's go get dinner." They made their way to the Cambria Pines Inn and sat outside by the fireplace. Each table was sectioned off by brick boundaries affording couples a quiet place to enjoy their romantic meal.

The food was delicious, and they both chose steak, asparagus covered in butter, sweet potatoes, and the finest champagne they had at the inn.

Just as they had finished their last bite, Scott reached into his pocket and gave her another one of his love letters. Harmony opened it slowly. What could this possibly be? What more surprises could my Scott have to give me?

When she had it opened, there was a key inside. Perplexed she looked at him and he chuckled, "Just wait, you will see tomorrow. I know you will be pleased. Right now, I want to hurry back to the room and continue with our bonding until the wee hours of the morning,"

Harmony giggled under her breath and turned a little pink around the cheeks.

Chapter Eleven

Home is Where the Heart is

The morning for the couple was midafternoon. They had spent the morning cuddling, talking, and making love. The Inn, hearing of their nuptials, catered a fabulous breakfast of bacon, eggs, toast, and fresh fruit.

"Shall we go for a walk along the beach and have lunch at the Moonstone Inn? I hear they have the best fish tacos."

"If you insist my husband," Harmony stretched and grabbed her summer clothes for their walk along the beach. "It's another beautiful day. I wish we had bought the land we looked at when we were up here so many years ago. I would love to have a little home here."

"Hurry my love, the sand awaits us. I have the same feelings as you do. It is beautiful, peaceful, and the perfect place to have a little retirement home."

The couple slowly walked for miles up and down the beach. They played catch with a young boy and his dog, and threw a Frisbee way over the head of a teenage couple, "Perhaps I need a little more practice" Scott laughed.

Harmony collected sand dollars and seashells to bring home to her grandchildren. They would be so surprised to find out she had gotten married. What would they think? Would they be upset that they weren't part of the ceremony or that they had not gotten a chance to get to know her newfound love?

"I know they will be happy for me that I have found happiness." Harmony accidentally said out loud.

"Who will be happy?" Scott asked.

"Everyone, especially the two of us!" Harmony said as she grabbed his hand and ran back to the car.

CHAPTER TWELVE

The Construction Begins

"There are so many pine trees here. I can see the ocean forever on the horizon. How did you ever find the perfect lot for us?" Harmony was twirling around and around trying to soak it all in.

After lunch, Scott had taken her for a drive up to the top of a hillside. On the drive he had given her a copy of the deed for the property he had bought in their favorite little town of Moonstone Beach.

"I'm sure you were wondering what I was doing after I sent you to the Queen Mary for New Year's Eve. I was busy driving up here looking for the most perfect piece of property I could find for our retirement house. I finally found it on top of this hill. I know how much you love the ocean and the pine trees. This is the perfect place for us to live the rest of our lives together." Scott grabbed her hand and they walked from one end of the property to the other.

"Yes, I was wondering what was happening when you didn't contact me. Now, I know. This is so amazing. The ocean, pine trees, and a hillside full of beautiful flowers." Harmony hugged Scoot so hard she started to cry. The cruel women had made her lose two homes. Now, she was going to have one to share with her love for the rest of her life.

When they had come up before, he talked about retiring up there with her. Sadly, she was being terrorized by those cruel women at the time. She was exhausted from trying to get the police to make them stop.

She had cried on the way home during the snowstorm, not wanting to go back to her house to live in fear. She had slept with a Taser and her phone under her pillow for years, never knowing when someone would hurt her. She had put alarms on her house, but they were still able to get into her home. One frightful night she had brought her granddaughter home to take her to a play and her house alarm did not work. Being a young child, her granddaughter mentioned that the alarm wasn't "talking" when they came in the garage door. They were tired and went to bed.

The alarm continued not working and Harmony's son-in-law came over to help her change the battery in her alarm system. They searched everywhere for the alarm box and finally found it in the garage.

"Harmony, there is no battery in the alarm system. We will have to buy a new one." Her son-in-law told her. "That's very strange. How could there not be a battery? I'll call the alarm company in the morning." The alarm company informed her of the exact date and time that her battery had been removed. Harmony discovered that this was just before she and her granddaughter had come home.

"They were in your house and took it out so they could come in and out whenever they wanted." These were some of the most chilling words Harmony had ever heard. She gave an involuntary shiver as she stood looking over at the ocean as she stood in the bright sunlight on the flowery hillside.

"Do you have a chill my love?" Scott held her closer and kissed her forehead. Harmony quickly changed the subject back to the present glorious moment. "I so love this place. Do you have plans already made up for our dream house?"

"Do you remember the night we stayed up talking about what our house would look like? We wanted three bedrooms. A master bedroom with a hot tub right outside, a bedroom for your grandchildren and children to visit and then an office for us. I wrote all those ideas down that night and kept them. I have given them to the architect and all we have left to do is pick out our colors, carpet, and tiles. Our beautiful retirement dream home will be ready in January."

"I can't wait! Thank you for fulfilling our dreams. But you need to promise me that there will be no alarm systems in this house."

Scott laughed lightly, "There is no need to be protected from evil anymore. It's just the two of us together forever." Scott walked back to the car and grabbed a blanket. Scott and Harmony cuddled together on their blanket of safety for hours, just basking in the togetherness and watching the sunset. Peacefulness surrounded them that night. This was a peacefulness that would stay with them forever.

When the sun set, the darkness prompted them to return to their hotel to make love over and over again. At one point, Harmony groggily asked, "What are we going to do for the rest of the year while our new house is being built?"

"Don't you worry about that my love, I have it all planned out" Scott answered as they both drifted off to sleep in each other's arms.

CHAPTER THIRTEEN

Castle in the Clouds

Harmony and Scott returned to his home in Redlands. It was a big, beautiful home on the top of the hill. This is where Scott had asked her to live with him when they first met. She so loved his house. It reminded her of her grandmother, Vernita. It was a classy home, filled with love. You could just feel the love between mother and son inside the house. When they were together, Harmony had spent many happy moments in this house. One of her favorites was on Mother's Day. Harmony had spent the morning with her children and then spent the afternoon and evening with Scott at his house. They had a movie marathon in the afternoon of Godzilla. Harmony loved Godzilla, she and her father had spent many years watching Godzilla movies when she was growing up. Who doesn't love Godzilla?

Harmony had always loved Scott's mom. She was a proper, intelligent woman who shared many family stories with her. She had been the one who told Harmony about the Church woman and the Barn Woman. Harmony had sent her gorgeous flowers and copies of her books to thank you for always being so kind to her when she needed it. When Harmony had first moved into the second house with security she had spoken to Scott's mom. She had given her a lot of further information about the Barn Woman. She was not happy with her and said that the Barn Woman was sending her son to their house to harass Scott. Painful memories at best, but the mother was a wonderful woman and beautiful to be around.

"How beautiful the stars are tonight." Harmony was relaxing in the hot tub with Scott looking up at the starry night." She suddenly started laughing.

"What is so funny? Did the bubbles tickle your funny bone?"

"I was just remembering the night we were in the hot tub, and it was thundering and lightning. Your mom was so worried about us. She kept coming out to get us until we went inside. I was not scared at all, but I loved her being worried about us so much. When we were swimming one day she kept coming out to talk to me. She had loaned me a book to read while we were bathing in the sunlight. She asked me all about my grandchildren. She told me I looked way too young to have so many. I wish she had gotten to meet them years ago."

"Yes, I am very lucky to have such a loving mother. I have been happy that I've been able to help her after my father died" Scott said as he held up the towel so that Harmony could go inside. "My favorite memory is when we were swimming, and I ran around naked to show you that our neighbors couldn't see us. You laughed at my antics of running around in my nakedness."

"You certainly did look super sexy in your nakedness. But I still only came out into the hot tub naked when it was dark!"

"Oh, you mean like tonight? I can't wait until we are inside, and I am covering every inch of you with my kisses.

"Sounds delightful!" Harmony ran inside to take a warm shower with her Scott. As they cuddled in bed, they spent the evening making love and planning a Memorial Day barbeque. Harmony and Scott wanted to have her children and grandchildren over for a swimming party. They had been so busy working on the new house, moving Harmony in, and caring for his mother, that they hadn't had a chance to properly introduce the newest member of the family.

"I am so excited that you finally get a proper meeting of my children and grandchildren!" said Harmony. "I love them so dearly and am proud of who they have become as adults. Our family time together has been so important to our family."

"I know I will love them as much as I love you. I can't wait to be a grandpa. My brothers are Grandpa's now so we can all share our experiences, and they can give me advice."

"My children will love you and welcome you into our family with open arms. If I am happy, they will be happy."

"Tomorrow I will go shopping for hamburgers, hot dogs, chips, sodas and water. We will also need to get a lot of pool toys for the grandchildren. I know the baby is learning to swim. I would love to help her. I wonder if they remember meeting me at your daughter's house when they had their weekly family get-together on Sundays watching The Walking Dead."

"I'm sure they will when they see you. Jonathan was just a baby then, now he is in 5th grade. I did not even like The Walking Dead. I would spend my time playing with my grandchildren. I loved our board games. Everyone has gotten so busy and things changed so much over the pandemic. We stopped doing that. I loved our monthly camping trips during the Pandemic so much. I wrote six children's books from our adventures. You will love venturing out with us."

"When I first met you I wanted to write children's books. Now, we can explore the world and write about our adventures together. I love finding new and unusual places and gathering details. I already have lots of ideas. You wanted to write a book on our adventures to the Valley of Fire and to Red Rock. That is first on our list. Nighty, night my love."

"Nighty, night!"

CHAPTER FOURTEEN

Splish-Splashing Fun

"Don't jump over your sister's head!"

"I wasn't even close!" Andy yelled as he did a back flip over his sister's head. He was the daredevil of the family. Though he did come by it honestly. His dad and Harmony's daughter had been together since childhood and many days were spent at the hospital as he was being repaired from one injury or another. Andy did so well while he was racing motorcycles when he was younger. The cruel evil people had snuck into Harmony's house and stole the money his parents had saved to buy him a new motorcycle. It broke his little heart at that time. He recently had fallen riding his bicycle down a mountainside and broken his back. It had healed and did not stop him at all from testing his skills by doing flips in midair.

Harmony smiled as she watched her new husband talking to her son and daughter, getting to know them. They had all come a long way in life. They had grown from young loves to parents of two of her grandchildren. Cameron had grown from a young man who did flips walking along the ocean waves to a welder putting together super-secret planes, her daughter worked with special needs children and then earned her degree in family counseling.

Her son was in the pool with the baby of the family. Olivia, or "Ollie", as she was known, was just turning three and learning to swim. She'd had a few issues when she was born but has grown into a feisty little girl with a lot to say and stubborn willpower. She was in good hands with her mommy the Registered Nurse and her daddy who was finishing his schooling as a middle school history teacher. Harmony wasn't surprised. She remembered him in middle school, failing his classes but staying after school to talk to his teachers. He loved learning, just not the formality, a rebel in his own right. Now, he was working with disadvantaged youth. You could feel the passion of his teaching when he spoke. His love for his family was very evident in the way he ran his life. Ollie's big sister, who has outgrown her nickname, Munchkin, was swimming underwater towards them to blow bubbles at her sister and tickle her.

Harmony's sultry grandson who had just graduated from high school was sitting in the lounge chair listening to his iPod protesting quietly coming to a family gathering. Harmony's oldest daughter fussed over him trying to get him to get into the pool. Harmony smiled at their interactions. She remembered when her children were teenagers. Being part of the family wasn't exactly the cool thing to do.

Harmony's other grandson Bryson was cautiously learning to dive from the side of the pool from Harmony's eldest granddaughter. "Just bend your body, point your arms, and push off of the side." Harmony could hear her giving him directions. "It's easy."

Bryson tried so hard to emulate what his cousin was showing him. He pointed his arms above his head, bent his little ten-year-old body, and pushed off the edge. His father Jace was waiting in the pool to catch him. There was a big splash as Bryson landed in the pool belly first. His dad swooped him up before he swallowed too much water. "You did an excellent job, Bryson!"

"I did it, I did it!" Bryson was so excited. "Yes, you did. Next time jump a little higher so you don't do a belly flop and splash water all over my face. I could hardly see you when you landed in the water!" Jace's arms were strong from years of welding but that didn't help if he couldn't see his son.

Jace and Harmony's older daughter had known each other since childhood also. Jace had spent many days at their house growing up. He had saved the family once by alerting them that a friend had run over the gas line and broken it. Harmony was very happy that they had gotten back together in their adulthood and had Bryson together. They were wonderful parents, with Harmony's oldest daughter working from home in the medical field for over twenty years. They had moved several hours away, and Harmony's ex-husband had moved back in with them after an illness. Harmony used to spend days at their home binge-watching reality TV with her daughter and relaxing. She so missed the closeness but knew they were doing their best to help her father. Today, was an extra special day for Harmony. Having all her children and grandchildren in one place celebrating her new life with her. Harmony was so very proud of all her children. Her heart was full.

"Dinner is ready! Come and get it!" Scott waved his spatula around in the air as it dripped with grease from the hamburgers. "We have cheeseburgers, hot dogs, and bratwurst for all!" Harmony gave her love a sparkling smile. She hadn't even seen him cooking the food. She was so enjoying her family's fun.

"We are so hungry. We are going to eat it all!" yelled Bryson as he pushed into the front of the line. It took no time at all for all the food to be eaten. Every single scrap of it. Harmony laughed because Scott had insisted on buying extra portions and he was so right.

With full tummies and a restful afternoon on the horizon, the children gathered chairs, drinks, and towels to sit at the outside table to play board games. A treasured moment for the family. They played a game just like Pictionary in which you had to draw a word and pass it down. A little like the telephone.

"What is this? It looks like an upside pickle on a chair!"

"It started as a rocket ship flying to the moon. I don't know what happened" laughed Harmony with her arms in the air. Her family always had so much fun playing this game together.

Suddenly, Scott came outside with his arms full of a box. "I have a surprise!" He placed the box down and started to hand everyone a lemonade with cotton candy on top! "I snuck out and went to the Spaghetti restaurant to get everyone a special surprise. When I first met Munchkin, I took her to dinner at her grandma's and my favorite spaghetti place. I bought a lemonade with cotton candy on top. I wanted to share that memory with all of Harmony's family. I think we should take our first family picture together with our cotton candy drinks!"

"An amazing idea. We will all stand in front of these beautiful purple flowers. This is my favorite spot in the backyard. I took a beautiful picture sitting on the couch looking out of the big picture window when I first met Scott."

Scott set up the camera and ran to stand next to his love Harmony. He had never had his heart as full of love as he was on this long-awaited day.

Harmony's thoughts roamed to that lovely picture she took of the backyard. Not knowing at that time that people were stalking her in her own backyard and the crazy women had watched them be together while they were intimate.

"Cheeseburger!" The camera snapped several times with the family taking several funny poses and then a serious one.

"Before everyone leaves, I want to invite you all to Florida with us. I know how much our family enjoys traveling and being together and I have planned a trip to Florida. Everyone has their own rooms and there are several waterslides inside the hotel. We will have an amazing time. "

"Wow! That's awesome!" The group chimed in together as they gave Harmony and Scott hugs and kisses.

It was soon time for each family to leave for home. "We will create a text chat for our upcoming trip to Florida!" the young ones yelled, already planning what they would pack for their trip.

CHAPTER FIFTEEN

Valley of Fire

Spring had moved into early summer and Harmony was so content with her new life. Especially since her family loved her new husband and all they could talk about was the upcoming trip to Florida.

"Pack your bags, Harmony. We have a trip to go on!" Harmony, never being one to argue about a trip, packed her bags and jumped in the car.

"Where are we going?"

"You wanted to write a book about Red Rock. This was something you asked me about several years ago. I wanted to return to our memories of our trip there and do some research for our book. I have all the spots mapped out." Scott brought out a map and a bag of hearts. "You wanted to put a heart at all of the places we went together and made love. You can keep yourself busy as we drive to Vegas tonight. Your wish is my command. I love you so much!"

Harmony gave Scott the biggest kiss and happily found the places on the map where they had been. The map was filling up very nicely. In the years to come, it was going to be overflowing with their happy trips. She wanted to get a world map and place hearts in every spot on the map that she could think of. The drive went quickly, and they were soon at their timeshare, an investment Harmony had received during her divorce and had built up. She and her family got another timeshare in Oceanside and spent weeks there during the late summer to celebrate her mother's birthday. It was their favorite family beach as her parents had owned a sailboat for over twenty years in the Oceanside Harbor.

Harmony took a short nap as they drove along. Her dream went back to when her children were young and she had talked her dad into taking them to Catalina. They sailed all night through the dark. Her young son had navigated during the night and found that it was harder than he thought and took much longer. Morning soon came and they anchored in the harbor at Avalon. They had to take a skiff to the beach from the sailboat. Harmony's father rented a golf cart, and they explored the island. It was a fabulous day for all involved. Those were the days of no cell phones. Harmony's father had called home to let his wife know where they were. Oh my, did they all get into trouble! Harmony's mother was not happy at all that they had taken the trip, so soon after the call, they all packed up and headed back home.

Harmony, not to be deterred, got her father to plan a trip to sail to Mexico when she was done working summer school. Sadly, her father passed away the week before this trip was to take place. Harmony especially treasured their sail to Catalina and all the memories it brought to her family. This was one reason she had the mural painted in her bedroom. Beautiful memories to wake up to.

"Are you ready?" Scott asked the next morning as he packed a picnic lunch of ham sandwiches, fruit, and water. "Ready when you are."

Harmony and Scott spent the day exploring the red rock of the Valley of Fire. Scott had picked a point on the road to walk down a gully and explore. They walked downhill for hours. Taking pictures, exploring the landscape, rock formations, and viewing the beautiful flowers. They hadn't realized they had walked that far and found they had a long trek uphill. Though Harmony was more than willing to walk up the road, Scott felt it was dangerous and went back to get the car. That is one of the many things that Harmony loved about Scott. His gentlemanly characteristics and his inability to get angry at her. Even when they were going through the worst of the stalking, Harmony was so upset. He never got upset with her. After the marriage she had been in this was a major plus for her, a man who was calm even under terrorizing circumstances. She always told him, "After everything these people have put us through, the rest of our lives will be like a walk in the park."

They climbed the ladder to see the petroglyphs that were etched in the Atlatl Rock walls. "These Petroglyphs were etched over 2,000 years ago," Scott explained to Harmony as she took pictures and notes. They had lunch in the Pastel Pink Canyon and took a long hike exploring all of the slot canyons along the white domes trail.

"Do you recognize this spot?" Scott asked her as he stopped along the side of the road. "I know how much you love Transformers. I wanted to show you where they were filmed."

"This is so beyond cool. You are so right! I love Transformers. I did not know they were filmed here. Now I can see this area in the film." Harmony planted a very wet kiss on Scott's mouth. She knew he was very special the first moment she met him. The fact that he remembered all the little things about her made her feel cherished and special.

"We have two more spots to see today. Can you walk anymore? I'd like to show you Rainbow Vista Trail and also Fire Canyon Overlook."

"Guide away, I can handle more exploring. I loved our day in the Red Rock Canyon. We are in no hurry to head home." Harmony and Scott continued to explore the Valley of Fire, reminiscing about their first trip together and gathering information for their children's book. Harmony had a special secret concerning her children's books, but she wanted to wait until it was solidified with a contract before giving Scott the big news.

"I'm ready to sit and have dinner. Where would you like to go?"

"I want to go back to Peggy Sue's where we went for dinner on our way home from our first trip to the Valley of Fire."

Peggy Sue's was a nostalgic restaurant in the middle of nowhere. Harmony was not really a desert fan, but her father had loved camping at Calico Ghost Town and Harmony had many loving memories of camping and stopping at Peggy Sue's on their way home.

"That is a wonderful idea. I loved it the first time we went, and I am so looking forward to cooling off and resting my tired toes. This was such an amazing day. I am so glad we came back to add to our memories of our trip here." Scott ordered the same meals they had on their first trip and they settled in to relax.

"I had such a wonderful time with you on our trip. Thank you for remembering that we were here and that I wanted to write a book on the park. The red rock is so beautiful. Look at the picture I took. It looks like a ghost face that the wind had etched into the red rock. I'm going to use it as the cover photo."

There Are Gators Everywhere!

The next few months flew by as Harmony and Scott were busy creating their children's book on the Valley of Fire. Harmony always loved his creative mind and herself following his lead in the ideas to add into the book. She knew they were going to have a wonderful life exploring the world and creating more books for the children of the world to learn from. Harmony started writing her books to help educate children and families on literacy, adventure, and friendship. She was beyond thrilled that Scott also had the same passions.

Their retirement house was coming along nicely, and they had taken several drives up the coast to check on the progress. It was beautiful and just what Harmony and Scott dreamed about. By the next year, they would be traveling up there frequently to walk along the boardwalk before breakfast, sitting by the ocean and listening to the waves, and watching the sunset as it ended another gorgeous peaceful day.

Then one day, they arrived at the airport to fly to Florida…

"I am so afraid to fly," Bryson was holding on to his mother's leg as they all waited to board the plane for their flight to Florida. Scott looked at his parents and then took Bryson's hand. "Come with me buddy, we are going to be airplane buddies. I promise you this is going to be such fun. We are going to eat your favorite pizza, get some peanuts, and watch the Transformers. Your grandma told me that you love Bumblebee. I've been watching all the movies with your grandma, and I agree with you. He is the coolest. Let's give the steward our ticket and get the show on the road."

Scott got Bryson all settled in his window seat and Harmony sat next to him. She gave his hand a squeeze and a silent thank you. Soon all fifteen of them were settled in their seats and the plane took off. True to his word Scott kept Bryson entertained and calm during the flight. He was even able to get the pilot to give him a quick tour of the cockpit so he could see who was flying them to their destination.

"That was super cool! Look the pilot gave me his cap and an airplane!" Bryson pretended to fly it as they departed the plane in Florida. You would think he'd never been nervous to fly.

Their family week began with a trip to Disneyworld. A day filled with rides, getting dizzy on the teacups, and wearing their poor feet out trying to keep up with the kids. The next few days were spent at the pool, relaxing and drinking cocktails with umbrellas in them for the adults.

"WWWOOOOO HHHHOOOO!" yelled Munchkin as she flew down the waterslide, landing in the pool butt first making such a big splash it got all the adults wet. Bryson and Andy soon followed suit with Andy landing headfirst into a dive off of the slide. The children were able to convince most of the adults to join them on the slide. The children took so many pictures of the adults plummeting off of the slide as ungracefully as possible.

"Thanks dad, I never thought I'd see you completely upside down with your pants hanging off your feet. You shocked the whole pool area!"

"Hey, the slide went faster than I thought. I didn't tighten my drawstring tight enough before I started down the slide. Don't show that picture to your friends!" He laughed as he chased his son around the pool trying to get his phone from him.

"Haha, it's way too late for that dad. Already sent!"

"Oh, man!" he laughed as he plopped down next to his wife and grabbed his fruity drink, poking his eye with the umbrella.

Their days were filled with fun in the sun and nights were filled with family game nights and laughter. Scott and Harmony excused themselves early to spend time alone. They were still in their honeymoon period and wanted to spend some quiet time together, though they fell asleep promptly after making love several times. This was one of the happiest times Harmony had ever had in her adult life. She wanted to show Scott how much she loved him and appreciated his planning their very special family trip.

Their last day in Florida was spent at the 1,000 Islands. They watched the dolphins playing in the wake of the boat for hours. They jumped in and out of the waves, taking turns flipping in and out of the water. The children were mesmerized by the fun antics of the dolphins. They almost forgot that the water was filled with alligators. They learned about the 1000 Islands, kayaked through the reefs, and visited alligator nests filled with baby eggs. It was a beautiful end to the week.

Scott and Harmony were alone in their room packing their bags for the plane ride home. "I bet we are going to write a book about our adventures this week," Scott chuckled.

"You guessed that right!" Harmony grabbed him and swung him onto the bed. "We have a few more minutes, what about curling my toes one last time before we head for home?"

"My pleasure! I'm going to make you giggle like you've never giggled before!" Scott groaned as Harmony began running her fingers through his chest hair and then followed his trail to his very special place. "Oh, Harmony, I am happier than I've ever been before. Don't stop now!"

Bang, bang, bang! The kids pounded on the door, "It's time to go to the airport!"

Harmony and Scott gathered themselves together, reluctantly, and opened the door.

Bryson was standing there gesturing for Scott to bend down. "Guess what?" he whispered to Scott.

"What?" Scott asked.

"I'm not afraid to fly anymore!"

"High five, buddy! That's great!"

CHAPTER SEVENTEEN

Christmas Day

The rest of summer passed quickly and Fall soon arrived. It had been such an amazing year for Harmony and Scott. Peaceful days and nights surrounded them in their home in Redlands. Scott's mom loved having Harmony around and told her all the stories of his childhood growing up in Redlands. Her closeness to Harmony came from their family trips. Her favorite story to tell was their trip to Africa. They went on Safaris and saw more animals than imaginable. Scott had talked to Harmony about taking her family there also. He wanted to share his family memories with her family. Harmony was hoping they could still venture around the world to a far-off land.

For the present, she was content living their quiet life in Redlands and enjoying the peace they had finally found. They had to fight hard to make the stalking and harassment stop. It was such a nightmare that they had lived through, but they came out of it closer and more in love than ever before. Evil never really wins.

They had a quiet Thanksgiving in the house and that night Harmony told Scott about her wish to have a big family Christmas at their house in Redlands.

"I think we can arrange that. Go ahead and start planning and I will invite my family. We haven't had a big family celebration here in such a long time. They will love it and love you." After kissing and hugging Scott, she ran and found the Christmas Wreath and hung it on the door.

Harmony spent the month between Thanksgiving and Christmas making Christmas cookies with her grandchildren and shopping with her eldest granddaughter who helped her wrap every single Christmas present that was placed under the tree.

One cold December evening, Harmony and Scott ventured to the Christmas tree farm to pick out the huge Christmas tree she wanted in her living room. "I want it to touch the ceiling!" They stopped at the entrance to the farm and bought steamy hot chocolate topped with whipped cream and just a hint of peppermint. "Just the thing I need to try to pick out our tree. There are so many choices!"

"Come and look at this one Harmony. It's perfect!" Harmony could hear his voice but had no idea where he had wandered off to. "Keep talking and I will follow your voice!"

To Harmony's surprise, Scott started singing the song she had dedicated to them. Her heart stopped for just a beat. When she first met him, she had gone to New Orleans. She took a picture of herself in front of a tattoo shop. He told her she was going to tattoo his name on her butt. Uh, NO, I'm not she thought. They continued to share text messages and pictures of her trip. Scott very lovingly told her, "You are having the time of your life."

Her heart caught and she opened just a little more to him. "No, I'm not with you." This song came from a love story she had loved as a teenager. They danced a famous dance at the end to "Time of My Life." The rebels show others how wrong they were about the true love between the characters in the movie.

Harmony followed his song and found him standing in front of the most magnificent pine tree she had ever seen. "It's just perfect my love."

"I will have them deliver it the night before Christmas Eve. That way we can all decorate it when our children and grandchildren come."

The baking was soon done, shopping and wrapping complete, menus were created, and several trips to the grocery store were made.

"They are here!" Harmony called Scott and his mom. "They're here!"

Harmony swung the door open and a rush of children, their parents, and bags and bags of presents and food entered the entryway. Harmony, Scott, and his mom hugged and kissed each and every one of them as they entered. For Harmony, this was a Christmas dream come true. She had not hosted a Christmas celebration since she was forced to sell her home. She missed it so much. All she wanted was to be surrounded by her family this first Christmas together for her and Scott.

Christmas Eve was filled with a yummy Turkey dinner with all the trimmings that Harmony's children had spent the day cooking. The smells filled the house as Harmony, Scott and his mother decorated the Christmas tree together. Scott's mom hadn't had a Christmas celebration in her home in a long time and was just as excited as Harmony was. Scott and Bryson hung the stockings on the mantel. There were so many it took over the whole fireplace.

Scott wanted one up for every person who would be there on Christmas morning, as he had a special gift to give to each of them.

The stockings were hung, the tree was trimmed, and their tummies were full. Scott made a fire to warm them on this chilly Christmas Eve. "Grandma read us our favorite story about "Queen Vernita's magical Christmas train ride. I love to remember our train ride to see Santa Claus!" Bryson ran over to give his grandma his favorite book.

"Of course, my love. That was such a memorable trip. Riding on the train in the snow to see the Grand Canyon and then Santa on the Polar

Express. You were so tired you fell asleep in Santa's lap!" The family gathered around Harmony as she read the Christmas tale. Scott watched with love as he listened. His mind wandered back to that trip. He couldn't go with Harmony, but she sent him many pictures. We should plan to take the family there next year at Thanksgiving, he thought as he made himself comfortable with Baby Ollie snuggled into him barely able to keep her eyes open.

Christmas morning came bright and early with the young ones ready to open their stockings and gifts from Santa. The noise woke Harmony and Scott, they put on their matching robes and slippers, their early Christmas presents to each other, and joined the family in the living room.

"What is this?" They all spoke at once as they took out a small envelope they each had in their stocking. Everyone had a mysterious golden ticket in their stocking.

"This is my Christmas present to everyone. I have read your grandma's Christmas train ride book many times. I was not able to go with you when you went many years ago, but this time I am going on the train ride with Santa with you. Next Thanksgiving we will all pack our pajamas and go together."

The children all jumped up to hug Scott. He was almost knocked over by the force of the happy children. His heart expanded so much at that moment that he thought it would burst with joy.

The rest of Christmas day was filled with laughter, the children playing with their Christmas gifts, and the adults planning their Thanksgiving trip, as well as lots of food. The day flew by and it was soon time for everyone to go home.

Harmony said, "Next year I would like to go to the Christmas Eve service in Wrightwood. I would like everyone to come with me. That church holds many memories for our family as we had your great-grandfather's service there."

They all promised to come as they kissed and hugged and thanked Scott for the wonderful Christmas gift.

"Harmony, do you hear that" Scott asked.

"Hear what? I don't hear anything."

"It's quiet now. I loved having everyone here. I'm so glad that our families were able to spend Christmas together this year. Our first year together with just peace and quiet. My family loved your family. I wish it hadn't taken so long for everyone to meet."

"Let's go to bed now my love. I have one last present for you. I know you are going to love it!"

"Lead the way My Queen. There is a reason you are called Queen Giggles!"

They made love in the hot tub that night, just as they had on many nights before they were reunited. Harmony drifted off to a restless sleep. In her dreams, Scott mentioned Queen Giggles had brought back why the storyline was created. It was a year after Harmony was forced out of her home. The evil women had stolen her emails and tried to get her fired from her teaching job. Harmony and her friend were sitting in the Sheriff's office trying to get help. The Sheriff was not happy with the church women. Harmony had given them evidence that she had called her realtor to find out where Harmony was moving to and who she was with. The Sheriff had stood in her living room telling her she couldn't stop the church woman and to never let her find out where she had moved to. It was such a frightening time in Harmony's life.

She let out a little cry in her sleep and Scott held her tighter. Her dreams went back to when she and her friend left the Sheriff's and traveled to Las Vegas for the weekend. On the way there they created a children's story titled Dragon's Breath. Harmony was Queen Giggles and Scott was King Teddy Bear. It was a lesson on not hurting others when you are angry or hurt.

Harmony's dream then returned to the phone call she and Scott shared while she read him her story. He is the one who named it Dragon's Breath. It was Harmony's way of processing what had happened to her in a healthy manner.

She woke up for a few minutes and stared at Scott sleeping soundly. She knew how lucky they were that they had lived through the darkness and still had each other. She closed her eyes and dreamed of Queen Giggles and King Teddy Bear's kingdom filled with flowers, meadows, love, and Precious the baby dragon. She smiled in her sleep as she dreamed of the grandest adventure of them all. Even in her sleep, she was excited for the good things to come. A place to call their own. A very special place to hang their Christmas Wreath.

Get Help for Stalking

Stalking is a public health problem that affects millions of people in the United States. Stalking involves a perpetrator's use of a pattern of harassing or threatening tactics that are both unwanted and cause fear or safety concerns in a victim.

Stalking tactics can include:

- Unwanted following and watching of the victim
- Unwanted approaching or showing up in places, such as the victim's home, workplace, or school
- Unwanted use of global positioning system (GPS) technology to monitor or track the victim's location
- Leaving strange or potentially threatening items for the victim to find
- Sneaking into the victim's home or car and doing things to scare the victim or let the victim know the perpetrator had been there
- Use of technology (e.g., hidden camera, recorder, computer software) to spy on the victim from a distance
- Unwanted phone calls, including hang-ups and voice messages
- Unwanted texts, emails, social media, or photo messages
- Unwanted cards, letters, flowers, or presents

Using technology to socialize and communicate has its conveniences, but it can also make it easier for people to harass others in ways that might be frightening and threatening.

Stalking is a public health problem that affects millions of people in the United States. Stalking involves a perpetrator's use of a pattern of harassing or threatening tactics that are both unwanted and cause fear or safety concerns in a victim.

Fast Facts: Preventing Stalking | Violence Prevention Injury Center | CDC

Fact Sheets & Infographics | Stalking Awareness & Prevention | SPARC

About the Author

Dr. Dawn Menge has won ninety international literacy awards and 200+ film festival awards as the published author of the Queen Vernita's Educational Series and Queen Giggles Kingdom, including the Special Recognition Champion Award from Conquering Disabilities with Film, Best Written Word from Miracle Makers Film, Hollywood Dreams Film, International Author Boss Award from Power Conversations Magazine and Success Magazine's 2023 Women of Influence. Presidential lifetime Achievement award 2024, 2X Author Allstars, Education 2.0 Excellence in Education award, International Association of Top Professionals let me say we are truly honored to have you as our Top Special Education Teacher & Author of the Decade. Her published works also include: THE SIX FEDERAL INDIVIDUAL EDUCATION PLAN GOALS AND THE EFFECTIVENESS OF THEIR IMPLEMENTATION IN PREPARING FOR TRANSITION.

Dr. Dawn Menge has a PHD in Education. She specializes in Curriculum and Instruction. She also holds a Master's and a Clear Credential in Moderate/Severe Disabilities and a Bachelor's Degree in

Human Development. Dr. Dawn Menge has been teaching students with severe cognitive delays for over twenty years, and mentors/lectures graduate students.

Dr. Dawn Menge is the mother of three, and the grandmother of six beautiful grandchildren.

LinkedIn: https://www.linkedin.com/in/menge-dr-dawn-72313419/
Facebook: http://www.facebook.com/dawn.menge1
Instagram: http://www.instagram.com/dawnmenge
Websites: http://www.landofquailshouse.com

One-on-One Writing Program with Dr. Dawn Menge

Join Dr. Dawn Menge, an esteemed educator with a Ph.D. in Education specializing in Curriculum and Instruction, for an exclusive one-on-one writing program. With a wealth of experience and expertise, Dr. Menge offers personalized guidance tailored to your individual needs and goals.

About Dr. Dawn Menge:

Dr. Menge brings over twenty-eight years of experience as an Education Specialist specializing in Severely Handicapped students for the San Bernardino County Superintendent of Schools. Her background includes working with students aged 3 to 22 with a diverse range of disabilities, including Autism, Down Syndrome, ADHD, Seizure Disorders, Orthopedic disorders, Mental illness, legally blind, and Cerebral Palsy. Her curriculum focuses on functional/vocational skills, empowering students to thrive within their community.

Dr. Menge is also a highly acclaimed author, having won twenty-nine national awards for her self-published Queen Vernita's Educational Series. Her series, recognized with a silver Mom's Choice Award, has garnered accolades from prestigious organizations such as Reader Views, Readers Favorites, First Place Evvy, Scooter Award, A+ rating from the American Children's Book Society, and multiple Purple Dragonfly awards.

In addition to her literary achievements, Dr. Menge has been honored with accolades such as Paraprofessional of the Year, Learning Leader from the Leapfrog Learning company, and nominations for Teacher of the Year for SBCSS. She has collaborated with the Leapfrog

Learning company on a Case Study focusing on her work with Autistic students and has been published in the Exceptional Parent Magazine and various online publications.

Program Highlights:

- *Personalized one-on-one sessions tailored to your writing goals.*
- Expert guidance from Dr. Dawn Menge, a seasoned educator and award-winning author.
- *Curriculum addressing your unique needs and skill level.*
- Proven strategies and techniques to enhance your writing proficiency.
- Ongoing support and mentorship to foster your growth as a writer.
- Access to Dr. Menge's extensive experience and insights in special education and literature.

Embark on a transformative writing journey with Dr. Dawn Menge and unlock your full potential as a writer. Whether you're a novice seeking to refine your skills or an experienced writer aiming to elevate your craft, **Dr. Menge's one-on-one program offers the personalized attention and expertise you need to succeed.**

https://landofquailshouse.com/programs
Go.landofquailshouse.com

Dr. Dawn Menge

The Inspiring Journey of Dr. Dawn Menge